Kosai

Slender Ella
AND HER FAIRY
Hogfather

To Sabrina
& Savannah

from [signature]
25 Dec 98

Slender Ella AND HER FAIRY HOGFATHER

by Vivian Sathre

illustrated by Sally Anne Lambert

A Yearling First Choice Chapter Book

To my sisters, Jeanette and Virginia,
who were never like Ruby and Pudge.
                            —V.S.

To my children, Jonny and Katie,
and to Sophie and Amy.
                    With love,
                    —S.A.L.

Published by
Bantam Doubleday Dell Publishing Group, Inc.
1540 Broadway
New York, New York 10036
Text copyright © 1999 by Vivian Sathre
Illustrations copyright © 1999 by Sally Anne Lambert
All rights reserved.

Library of Congress Cataloging-in-Publication Data
Sathre, Vivian.
  Slender Ella and her Fairy Hogfather / by Vivian Sathre ; illustrated by
Sally Anne Lambert.
    p. cm.
  Summary: Slender Ella, a pig forced into servitude by her stepmother and
two horrid stepsisters, goes to the hoedown with the help of her Fairy Hogfather
and marries the handsome son of the Goldsnoots of Diamond Snout Hay Ranch.
  ISBN 0-385-32516-9 (hc). —ISBN 0-440-41397-4 (pb).
  [1. Pigs—Fiction. 2. Humorous stories.]   I. Lambert, Sally Anne, ill.
  II. Title.
PZ7.S24916Sl   1999
[E]—DC21   CIP
                                                          AC

Hardcover: The trademark Delacorte Press® is registered in the U.S. Patent and
                    Trademark Office and in other countries.
Paperback: The trademark Yearling® is registered in the U.S. Patent and
                    Trademark Office and in other countries.

Visit us on the Web! www.bdd.com
Educators and librarians, visit the BDD Teacher's Resource Center at
www.bdd.com/teachers

The text of this book is set in 17-point Baskerville.
Manufactured in the United States of America
April 1999
10   9   8   7   6   5   4   3   2   1

Contents

❦ ① ❦
Home Sweet Home

Once upon a time
a sweet little pig named Ella
lived with her father.
Then Father Pig got married again.
His new wife and her two daughters
were very mean.

Father Pig was a traveling salesman
and was away from the ranch
more days than he was home.
So Ella got all the meanness
those steppies dished out.

"What a skinny runt you are,"
said Ruby, the older stepsister.
Pudge, the younger stepsister, agreed.
"Let's call her Slender Ella."
The two pigs laughed.
"Now fix us lunch," ordered Pudge.
"You might say *please*," said Slender Ella.

"Fat chance," said Ruby.
After lunch Slender Ella started
down the root cellar stairs
to her room.

9

"Not so fast," said her stepmother.

"Clean up this mess."

"But I didn't make the mess,"
Slender Ella said.

"Don't get snouty with me,"
Stepmother Pig warned.

"I said *clean it up.*"

So Slender Ella scrubbed
and polished late into the night.

First thing the next morning
Stepmother Pig handed Slender Ella
a basket of dirty clothes.
"Before you plow the fields,
make the beds and do the laundry."
Slender Ella sighed.

11

Plowing was the only fun thing
she ever got to do.
The wind blowing in her face
made her feel wild and free.
And no one was there to
order her around.

That afternoon the mailman came by.
He handed Stepmother Pig
an envelope.
She read it, then said,
"The Goldsnoots
of the Diamond Snout Hay Ranch
are having a fancy hoedown.

Their son, Harley Joe,

is looking for a wife.

And we're invited!"

"Wowzer!" Slender Ella said, smiling.

"Not *you*," said her stepmother.

Ruby snorted. "Why would the son

of a fancy-shmancy rancher want

a skinny-bones like you

when he could have me?"

"Or *me*." Pudge frowned at Ruby.

Slender Ella turned away.

Her steppies were right.

She was just a skinny runt

in ragged clothes.

2
Poof!

The next day Slender Ella helped
her stepsisters get ready
for the hoedown.
"Shine my shoes!" Ruby ordered.
"Oh, thorns! Make my dress roomier,"
Pudge demanded.

Slender Ella ran back and forth
trying to please her stepsisters.
"You both look lovely," she said.
"We'll have a ball," Ruby said.
"I can't wait to see who
Harley Joe picks," said Pudge.
"I'm sure he'll choose one
of my beauties," their mother snorted.

And with that, the three steppies

swept out the door.

Slender Ella followed them out.

She sniffed and sat down.

She picked a dandelion puff.

Then she closed her eyes.

"I wish I could go to the dance too!"

Slender Ella blew on the puff.

When she opened her eyes

the dandelion seeds were sparkling.

Then, *poof!* They disappeared.

A stout pig stood before Slender Ella.

He removed his hat and bowed.

"Your Fairy Hogfather

at your service."

"Wowzer!" Slender Ella exclaimed.

"You can go to the dance," he said.

"But you must be home by midnight."

He waved his walking stick

and her shabby clothes

turned into a flouncy party dress.

She spun around. "Ooh-la-la.

All these ruffles give me

a full-figured look."

He waved his walking stick again.

Diamond-studded cowboy boots

appeared on Slender Ella's feet.

"Come, it's time for you to go,"

her Fairy Hogfather said.

He turned toward the field.

Another wave of his walking stick
turned the tractor into a shiny car.
Slender Ella gasped. "For me?"
He nodded and changed a firefly
into her driver.

"Remember, at the stroke of twelve
everything returns to what it was."

"I'll remember," Slender Ella said.

Her hogfather bowed.

Then, *poof!* He disappeared.

❧ 3 ❧
Round and Fat

When Slender Ella glided
into the Diamond Snout hay barn,
everyone stopped and stared.
"She's beautiful!" they whispered.
"Who could she be?"

Even her steppies didn't know her.

Then Slender Ella saw Harley Joe.

He was the roundest,

fattest pig she'd ever seen.

It was love at first sight for her.

And Harley Joe was walking her way!

He tipped his studded hat.

"Howdy. May I have this dance?"

"Sure thing," said Slender Ella.

Her heart pounded like hoofbeats.

They danced to song after song.
"Where y'all from?" he asked
as they two-stepped
to "Sweet Adel-Swine."
"Near," said Slender Ella.

Suddenly a pig in a red dress tapped
Slender Ella on the shoulder.
"Quit hogging Harley Joe."
She bumped Slender Ella aside.

But the very next song Harley Joe
trotted back to Slender Ella's side.
All night long pig after pig cut in
to dance with him.
But Harley Joe always came back
to Slender Ella.

"Why haven't I seen y'all
before tonight?" he asked.
"I'm a very busy pig," she replied.
Bong! . . . *Bong!* . . . *Bong!*
Slender Ella looked up at the clock.
It was striking midnight!
"Good night!" Slender Ella cried.

She turned and ran so fast
she tripped over her own feet.
One of her boots flew off.
Harley Joe picked it up.
"Wait!" He raced after her
but was caught in the crowd.
Slender Ella reached the car
at the last stroke of twelve.

Pop! The car changed back to a tractor.

Pop! Her driver became a firefly.

Pop! She was in her old clothes.

The only thing left

of her lovely evening was

one diamond-studded cowboy boot.

She jumped up onto the tractor

and drove home.

Later, when her steppies came in,

Slender Ella ran to the door.

"How was the hoedown?" she asked,

eager to hear more about Harley Joe.

Ruby and Pudge giggled.

"Wouldn't you like to know?"

Then they began to whisper.

But only to each other.

4
Double Thorns

The next morning Ruby and Pudge
woke Slender Ella early.

"I'm hungry," said Pudge.

"Make our breakfast and *maybe*
we'll tell you about last night."

"Harley Joe is *very* charming,"
Ruby said.

Slender Ella sighed.

She thought so too.

Slender Ella hurried to the kitchen.

Just as she began cooking flapjacks,

someone knocked at the door.

"Answer that, Slender Ella,"
ordered Stepmother Pig.

Slender Ella opened the door.

Wowzer! It was Harley Joe.

He looked even fatter than before.

Slender Ella's heart fluttered.

Harley Joe removed his hat.

"Howdy."

He held out the diamond-studded boot.

"So far I've asked half the ladies
in the county to try on this boot.

It didn't fit a one." He smiled.

"Would y'all mind trying it on?

I hope to marry the sweet potato
who belongs to this boot."

Ruby pushed forward. "Me first."
She squeezed and crammed
but the boot would not go on.
"My foot must be a little puffy
from all the dancing," she grunted.

Pudge nudged her sister
out of the way. "My turn."
She wiggled and jiggled and stomped.
But she had no better luck than Ruby.
"Oh, thorns! I must have eaten
too many berry tarts last night."

Slender Ella stepped forward.

"The boot belongs to me," she said.

"Hogwash!" said Stepmother Pig.

"You didn't even go to the dance."

Slender Ella lifted her foot.

The boot slipped right on.

She pulled out the matching boot.

The steppies gasped.

"Double thorns," Pudge grumbled.

"Now she'll be rich and get

to live high on the hog."

Harley Joe kneeled by Slender Ella.

"Will you marry me?" he asked.

Slender Ella smiled.

"Wowzer! You bet." She paused.

"But will you promise to let me plow
all the fields on your ranch?"
Harley Joe nodded.
"Whatever you say, my sweet potato."

The whole county was invited
to the wedding.
"I'm so happy for you," Father Pig said.
And Slender Ella's stepsisters
were much nicer now.

They became her maids and moved
to the Diamond Snout Hay Ranch.
Slender Ella loved the fancy tractor
Harley Joe gave her
for a wedding present.
"You treat me like a princess,"
she told Harley Joe. And he did.

46

Every day he sang her love songs
and cooked her a big meal
when she came in from the fields.
Slender Ella grew to be
quite a well-rounded pig.
She and Harley Joe
lived happily ever after.

About the Author

Vivian Sathre is also the author of *Leroy Potts Meets the McCrooks*. She lives in Washington state.

About the Illustrator

Sally Anne Lambert has illustrated many children's books, including *Too Close Friends*. She lives in England.